P9-CCV-607

Millions of Americans remember Dick and Jane (and Sally and Spot too!). The little stories with their simple vocabulary words and warmly rendered illustrations were a hallmark of American education in the 1950s and 1960s.

But the first Dick and Jane stories actually appeared much earlier—in the Scott Foresman Elson Basic Reader Pre-Primer, copyright 1930. These books featured short, upbeat, and highly readable stories for children. The pages were filled with colorful characters and large, easy-to-read Century Schoolbook typeface. There were fun adventures around every corner of Dick and Jane's world.

Generations of American children learned to read with Dick and Jane, and many still cherish the memory of reading the simple stories on their own. Today, Pearson Scott Foresman remains committed to helping all children learn to read—and love to read. As part of Pearson Education, the world's largest educational publisher, Pearson Scott Foresman is honored to reissue these classic Dick and Jane stories, with Grosset & Dunlap, a division of Penguin Young Readers Group. Reading has always been at the heart of everything we do, and we sincerely hope that reading is an important part of your life too.

CHASE BRANCH LIBRARY
17731 W. SEVEN MILE RD.
DETROIT, MI 48235
578-8002

MAY 10

CH

GROSSET & DUNLAP
Published by the Penguin Group
Penguin Group (USA) Inc., 375 Hudson Street, New York, New York 10014, U.S.A.
Penguin Group (Canada), 10 Alcorn Avenue, Toronto, Ontario, Canada M4V 3B2
(a division of Pearson Penguin Canada Inc.)
Penguin Books Ltd, 80 Strand, London WC2R 0RL, England
Penguin Ireland, 25 St Stephen's Green, Dublin 2, Ireland
(a division of Penguin Books Ltd)
Penguin Group (Australia), 250 Camberwell Road, Camberwell, Victoria 3124, Australia
(a division of Pearson Australia Group Pty Ltd)
Penguin Books India Pvt Ltd, 11 Community Centre, Panchsheel Park,
New Delhi - 110 017, India
Penguin Group (NZ), Cnr Airborne and Rosedale Roads, Albany, Auckland 1310, New Zealand
(a division of Pearson New Zealand Ltd)
Penguin Books (South Africa) (Pty) Ltd, 24 Sturdee Avenue, Rosebank,
Johannesburg 2196, South Africa

Penguin Books Ltd, Registered Offices:
80 Strand, London WC2R 0RL, England

The scanning, uploading, and distribution of this book via the Internet or via any other means
without the permission of the publisher is illegal and punishable by law. Please purchase only
authorized electronic editions, and do not participate in or encourage electronic piracy of
copyrighted materials. Your support of the author's rights is appreciated.

Dick and Jane™ is a trademark of Pearson Education, Inc.
From THE NEW WE WORK AND PLAY. Copyright © 1956 by Scott, Foresman and Company,
copyright renewed 1984. From WE READ PICTURES. Copyright © 1951 by Scott, Foresman and
Company, copyright renewed 1979. From WE READ MORE PICTURES. Copyright © 1951 by
Scott, Foresman and Company, copyright renewed 1979. From THE NEW BEFORE WE READ.
Copyright © 1956 by Scott, Foresman and Company, copyright renewed 1984. From THE NEW
WE COME AND GO. Copyright © 1956 by Scott, Foresman and Company, copyright renewed
1984. All rights reserved. Published by Grosset & Dunlap, a division of Penguin Young Readers
Group, 345 Hudson Street, New York, NY, 10014. GROSSET & DUNLAP is a
trademark of Penguin Group (USA) Inc. Printed in the U.S.A.

Library of Congress Control Number: 2003016831

ISBN-13: 978-0-448-43410-0 (pbk)                                    I J
ISBN-13: 978-0-448-43496-4 (hc)                         B C D E F G H I J

ALL ABOARD READING™

Station Stop 1

# Dick and Jane

# We Play

Grosset & Dunlap

# Table of Contents

# Play

Oh, Father.
See funny Dick.
Dick can play.

Oh, Mother.
Oh, Father.
Jane can play.
Sally can play.

Oh, Father.

See Spot.

Funny, funny Spot.

Spot can play.

# See Dick Play

Look, Jane.

Look, look.

Look and see.

See Father play.

See Dick play.

Look, Mother.

Look, Mother, look.

See Father.

See Father and Dick.

Oh, Mother.

See Spot.

Look, Mother, look.

Spot can help Dick.

# Funny Spot

Come Spot.
Come, come.
Play Spot.
Play, play.

Go, Spot.
Go, go.

Spot can play.

Dick can play.

Oh, oh.

Funny, funny Spot.

# See Spot Play

See Jane jump.

Jump, jump.

See Spot jump.

Jump, jump.

Oh, Dick.
Oh, Jane.
See Spot.

Funny, funny Spot.

Spot can play.

# Funny Father

"Come, Jane," said Father.
"Come and play ball.
Come and play."

"I can help you play ball," said Father.

"I can help."

"Come, Father," said Jane.
"Come and play ball.
Come and play."

Oh, funny, funny Father.

# Play Ball

"Come, Jane," said Father.
"Come and play ball.
Come and play."

"Oh," said Jane.
"See the red ball go.
See it go up, up, up.
Run, Dick, run."

"Oh, oh," said Dick.

"Where is my ball?

I can not find it.

Come here, Jane.

Run and help me.

Help me find my red ball."

"I can help you," said Jane.

"We can find the red ball."

Dick said, "I see it.
I see my red ball.
Look, Father.
See where it is.
Come and help me."

Jane said, "Oh, Dick.
Spot can help you.
Spot can find the ball."